ALL ABOARD!

BY JAMES STEVENSON

GREENWILLOW BOOKS, NEW YORK

For Matthew

Watercolor paints and a black pen were used for the full-color art. The text was hand-lettered by the author.

Copyright © 1995 by James Stevenson. All rights reserved. No part of this book may be reproduced or utilized in any form or by any means, electronic or mechanical, including photocopying, recording, or by any information storage and retrieval system, without permission in writing from the Publisher, Greenwillow Books, a division of William Morrow & Company, Inc., 1350 Avenue of the Americas, New York, NY 10019. Printed in Hong Kong by South China Printing Company (1988) Ltd.   First Edition   10 9 8 7 6 5 4 3 2 1

LIBRARY OF CONGRESS CATALOGING-IN-PUBLICATION DATA
Stevenson, James [date]
All aboard! / by James Stevenson.
p.   cm.
Summary: Hubie and his family take the Broadway Blazer to the 1939 World's Fair,
but Hubie gets off and has a series of adventures.
ISBN 0-688-12438-0 (trade).   ISBN 0-688-12439-9 (lib bdg.)
[1. Mice—Fiction.   2. Railroads—Trains—Fiction.   3. Adventure and adventurers—Fiction.]
I. Title.   PZ7.S84748A1   1995   [E]—dc20   94-5825   CIP   AC

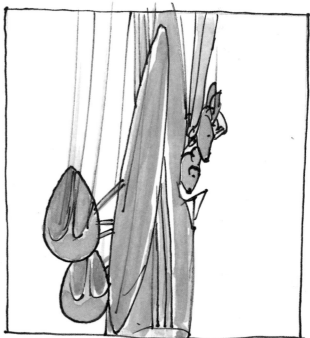